THIS DIARY BELONGS TO

chloe

Dear Riders,

A warm welcome to Sunnyside Stables!

Sunnyside is our home and for the next week it will be yours too! We're a big family — my husband Johnny and I have two children, Millie and James, plus two dogs ... and all the ponies, of course!

We have friendly yard staff and a very talented instructor, Sally, to help you get the most out of your week. If you have any worries or questions about anything at all, just ask. We're here to help, and we want your holiday to be as enjoyable as possible — so don't be shy!

As you know, you will have a pony to look after as your own for the week. Your pony can't wait to meet you and start having fun! During your stay, you'll be caring for your pony, improving your riding, enjoying long country hacks, learning new skills and making friends.

And this week's special activity is a challenging treasure hunt. Just imagine you and your pony cantering across the countryside together, solving clues! Add swimming, games, films, barbecues and a gymkhana and you're in for a fun-filled holiday to remember!

This special Pony Camp Diary is for you to fill with all your holiday memories. We hope you'll write all about your adventures here at Sunnyside Stables — because we know you're going to have lots!

Wishing you a wonderful time with us!

Jody xx

Monday morning
– at Pony Camp!

Jody, the lady who runs Sunnyside Stables, gave me this cool diary when I arrived just now. Her letter at the front says it's to write down all the adventures I have this week. It's fantastic here – there are two outdoor manèges and lots of cute ponies and dogs everywhere and even a swimming pool! I'm hoping to have lots of adventures – especially jumping ones!

I really wanted to come on this week because when Mum rang up and spoke to Jody, she said they're holding a special jumping competition on the last day. In our lessons, we're going to work on building up to an eight-jump course, and it's even going to include some cross-country fences for fun – I can't wait!

I love jumping but I've only done a couple of smaller courses at clear round events at my local riding school. I'm really hoping to improve while I'm here – and I'm desperate to go clear in Friday's competition.

The reasons I want a clear round so much are:

a. because I've never had one before
so it will be a big
challenge for me and
b. to make Dad proud of me.

Although Dad knows how much I love ponies (I'm always talking about getting my own one day!), he's never actually seen me ride. He's always working, even at weekends. But he said he'll really, really try to come with Mum to pick me up on Friday, then he'll be able to see me in the jumping competition and I can amaze him with my clear round (fingers crossed!). I really hope he keeps his word and doesn't get stuck at work as usual.

Jody

Sally

As soon as I got here, I kept asking Jody what we'll be doing every day because I was really excited. She smiled and said Sally, the instructor, will explain that when everyone arrives, but I really, really wanted to know straight away so she gave me a copy of the timetable to stick into my diary. She has warned me that it will change, though, because we have special activities on some days. Like, it says in her letter we're going on a treasure hunt this week – that sounds really fun!

Sunnyside Stables

Here's the timetable for the week:

Pony Camp Timetable

8am: Wake up, get dressed, have breakfast

8.45am: Help on the yard, bring in the ponies from field, muck out stables, do feeds, etc.

9.30am: Prepare ponies for morning lessons (quick groom, tack up, etc.)

10am: Morning riding lesson

11am: Morning break - drink and biscuits

11.20am: Pony Care lecture

12.30pm: Lunch and free time

2pm: Afternoon riding lesson

3pm: Break - drink and biscuits

3.20pm: Pony Care lecture

4.30pm: Jobs around the yard (i.e. cleaning tack, sweeping up, mixing evening feeds, turning out ponies)

5.30pm: Free time before dinner

6pm: Dinner (and clearing up!)

7pm: Evening activity

8.30pm: Showers and hot chocolate

9.30pm: Lights out and NO TALKING!

Wow! There's so much to do here! I just can't wait to find out which pony I'm getting – having my own pony to look after for a whole week will be fab!

This morning we're having an assessment lesson where we all ride in together, and then Sally will decide who goes in which group. So the timetable's different already because there's no lecture this morning. It's now 10.35am and not everyone is here yet, including the girls who are sharing my room – but, oh, now I can hear talking and clumping on the stairs. Maybe it's them!

Two minutes later

It *was* them!

The two girls I'm sharing with have gone downstairs to help on the yard – we are all still waiting for a couple of others to arrive, but the adults keep telling each other that there's a hold-up on the M3 so we're running a bit later than planned.

I'm going down in a minute but first I just wanted to do a quick profile of my room-mates for my diary.

Name: Isabella

Age: 12

Lives: Buckinghamshire, which is sort of near to London but still in the countryside.

Description: Quite tall for 12,

goes to a school for girls only, has amazing green eyes and long wavy brown hair and plays the cello and has packed three different swimsuits because she couldn't decide which to bring (I've only *got* one!). She says her friends call her Bella, and we can too (how cool!).

Name: Georgia

Age: 12

Lives: Georgia comes all the way from Devon, which I suppose isn't actually far from here, but it's a long way from where I live (i.e. London).

Description: Short blondish hair. She seems very sensible and mature for 12, but she's also really friendly so that's okay. She has two younger brothers and one younger sister and says she has to help her mum and dad look after them quite a lot.

The best thing is that Isabella and Georgia are both really into jumping too and they also chose this week specially to come to Sunnyside, so they could spend lots of time focussing on it. Also, they're both really nice and are not leaving me out just because I'm a weeny bit younger than them, which older girls can sometimes do.

Oh, I have to go – Bella's calling me down to the yard. Maybe it's time to find out which ponies we're getting. I'm so excited just thinking about it! Fingers crossed mine's a good jumper!

Still Monday morning,

in our break

I am quickly writing this because I've got something exciting to put down that can't wait till later. The girls who were delayed are here now and we're just about to have our assessment lesson. But even though we haven't been given our ponies yet I have already met the perfect one for me.

What happened was, when I got outside, Jody explained that while we were waiting for the last two girls to arrive, we could get on with some yard work. She gave me mucking-out duty with this really nice stable girl called Lydia. That's when I met Charm, who is an amazingly gorgeous grey Connemara.

Sunnyside Stables

I fell in love with him straight away and Lydia
said I could lead him out and tie him up in the
yard while we did his stable. I gave him a big
stroke and pat on the way and he whinnied and
nuzzled into my T-shirt.

While we were working I asked Lydia about
him and she told me what a great
jumper he is. That just made me
want him to be my pony even
more!

Lydia

When Lydia and I had put the
new straw down on top of the
clean bits of bedding and spread it
all out, I got to lead Charm back in,
and I whispered to him that I really
hoped he'd be my pony for the
week. After a while, the other girls
arrived and Jody called us all back into the main
yard and introduced us to each other and the
Sunnyside Stables team.

18

As well as me and Bella and Georgia there is Millie, Jody's daughter, who I read about in the welcome letter. The girls sharing her room are called Suki and Mai and they go to an international school in London. They are both eight and three-quarters and are actually from Japan.

Suki   Mai

Then there are the little ones, Olivia, Asha and Joelle (who is only just seven and the youngest of all), and they're in a room together.

Asha

Joelle

Olivia

Me, Bella and Georgia are all really excited about the jumping and we're crossing our fingers that we get put in the group to do it. Bella and Georgia have jumped a bit but neither of them have done a competition yet, so I've probably got the most experience, even though it's not much.

I really, really hope I've got Charm. I've worked out I've got a 33.3333333333% chance of getting him – he's a bit big for the younger girls and Millie has her own pony, of course, and so I reckon it will be between me, Georgia and Bella.

Still Monday,
after the ponies were given out

Well, it didn't exactly go as I'd hoped, but I'm trying not to be too disappointed. We were all waiting in the yard with our hats and crops and everything, and Sally was reading from a list while Lydia brought the ponies out, one by one. They were already tacked up, because some of the girls had been helping do that while I was mucking out.

I was really excited and as Lydia led Charm out I had all my fingers crossed for luck, but then Sally said, "Isabella, you're on Charm. I hope you two will hit it off. Charm's a superb jumper, and he has lovely manners." Well, my heart sank and I had to blink fast to stop tears coming into my eyes. Bella looked so excited and I forced myself to smile at her.

Bella thanked Sally and stroked Charm's nose before leading him over to the mounting block. As he nudged her shoulder happily, I couldn't help thinking that he should have been nudging *my* shoulder instead.

Then Sally said, "Chloe, you've got Cracker. He's a really spirited, cheeky little thing so you'll need all your experience!" She didn't mention his great jumping or good manners, but he is quite sweet, I suppose – a grey Welsh Section B, with big eyes and a cute pink bit on his nose. Lydia says he's 12.2hh and I feel a bit big for him – my heels are almost off his sides. Charm's over a hand higher. I just wish ... but there's no point in wishing. I haven't got Charm so I'll just have to try and make the best of it. I don't want to waste my holiday moping!

I'll write about the assessment lesson in a minute, but first here's my drawing of who got which pony:

Sunnyside Stables

Bella - Charm,
my fave!

Georgia - Prince,
a really sweet
cobby piebald

Mai - Star

Olivia - Ebony

Me - Cracker!

Joelle - Monsoon

Asha - Sugar

Suki - Twinkle

Millie is riding her pony,
Tally, of course.

Sunnyside Stables

We had the assessment lesson and it went okay. Millie didn't ride with us – Jody said she had to get on with her holiday homework instead. Poor thing!

At first we just had to walk and trot and think about our position and making good transitions. Then we did some turns and circles and changes of rein, and at the end we all had a canter to the back of the ride, except Joelle 'cos she hasn't done much riding and she only knows walk and trot at the moment. Instead, she turned Monsoon into the middle and Sally held on to her while we cantered on one rein and then the other.

Sally was right about Cracker, he is quite cheeky. I really had to keep my inside leg on all the way round or he'd fall in off the track, and when I just gently used my crop to get him listening (he wasn't going into trot for anyone!) he did a couple of little bucks. I didn't really mind, but I tried not to look at Bella trotting round perfectly on Charm, or at their lovely effortless transitions, which didn't involve any kicking or flailing arms like mine did.

Afterwards we put our ponies back in the stables (or in pens in the big barn for the ones who live out) and untacked. I gave Cracker a brush down and made sure he had enough water. Then we came back into the yard and gathered round Sally to hear the news.

Here are the groups we're in:

Group A: Suki, Mai, Olivia, Joelle, Asha.
Group B: Me, Bella, Georgia, Millie.

Our group will be doing the jumping and entering the clear round comp at the end of the week! Group A is the less experienced group, and on Friday they're going to do gymkhana games instead of jumping the course. Sally told them they'll still get to have a go at jumping in their lessons so they won't be missing out.

When we heard that
we were doing the
jumping comp, Bella
grabbed me and
Georgia and we all
leaped up and down in a
huggy group.

I was excited of course, but not as much as I
pretended to be. I mean, I know it's not Bella's
fault she got given Charm and I didn't, but I really,
really wish I had him.

I thought I would've forgotten about Charm
by now – but I just can't seem to. I'll have to
make sure I hide how I feel. I don't want to fall
out with my new friends when I've only just met
them! Maybe things will be better after the first
jumping lesson, when we've made a start and I'm
on my way to getting that clear round. Now I've
got a handle on Cracker's bad habits I'll be a
whole lot stricter!

Monday 6.32pm
In our room

We're going swimming tonight for our evening
activity, but Jody says we have to let our tea go
down for half an hour first. We're all squashed
on to the top bunk, which is Georgia's (Bella is
below and I am in the single bed by the
window), writing in our diaries. We were up
here talking before but Bella kept
going on and on about how
amazing Charm is, and it was really
getting on my nerves, so I
suggested we did some writing
instead.

This afternoon it was really scorching hot so
Sally said we'd have our Pony Care lecture first
and then have our riding lesson afterwards
when it was cooler. She showed us how to tie

27

the ponies up correctly and where all the equipment goes so we don't leave anything lying about that could be a danger, and what to wear and everything.

Then after the break we had our first jumping lesson. I was so excited! We had a warm-up for about twenty minutes, working in all the paces on each rein. When we stopped to put our stirrups up a couple of holes, Georgia got worried that Sally was going to start setting up the course right away. But Sally explained that we'll be starting with trotting poles and singles and then building up gradually, so Georgia felt okay after that.

We did some basic pole work, then we practised trotting on and going into the jumping position down the long side, which was quite tricky. Cracker enjoyed it because I didn't exactly have all my powers of steering in that position and so he got to cut the corner off and wander across the manège!

Then Sally set up a simple cross pole. First we approached in trot (except Millie, because Tally just charged at it in canter!). After a couple of goes we came up in trot and then cantered away, and we had to keep the canter till we reached the back of the ride. Cracker cut the corner off the first time, but after that I got my inside leg on straight after the jump so he had to behave. There's so much to think about with him on just one jump, I have no idea how I'm going to get round a whole course!

Then we cantered the whole thing and he cut the corner off again before I even had time to think. I got a bit annoyed with him and felt like giving up. It must have showed because Sally called out, "He's perfectly capable, Chloe, he's just seeing what he can get away with.Circle him round and go again." Then when I went over the next time, she shouted

least I kept him on the track down the short
side, although I bet I looked really clumsy and
unseated.

I've just moved over a bit to make sure Bella
can't see what I'm writing. I feel really bad even
putting this down, but I have to because it's
what happened. We finished off the lesson by
working over a double, and Sally made the
second pole into an upright. Cracker did okay,
but he only just cleared it, whereas Charm

Not fair!

sailed miles over and I felt really
jealous again. I bet Bella will
go clear in the comp
without even trying and
she's probably not even that
bothered whether she
does or not! I bet here
dad makes a big fuss of her whatever
she does. It just doesn't seem fair that I really
need Charm and she's got him.

that I really need Charm and she's
got him.

Oh, I feel awful and I wish I
hadn't put that now. It's not Bella's fault she got
Charm. I hate feeling this way – it's just not like
me at all. Right, I'm going to climb down from
here right this second and hide this diary
somewhere in my stuff.

And then I'm going to try my hardest to
forget all about Charm.

Tuesday lunchtime

We've just had lunch and I'm sitting outside on the benches in the sun.

I was going to write in here when we went to bed last night (I've got a cool little torch on my key ring) but after two lots of riding, then swimming as well, I'd run out of energy. Still, even though we were all tired, we kept bursting into giggles after lights out because Bella was whispering this story to us about a boy down her road who keeps asking her out. Georgia and Bella are brilliant fun – I'm so glad I'm sharing a room with them!

This morning we had our Pony Care lecture on tack and tacking up. I knew some of it already, but it was really good to learn about all the different bits. Also, Lydia was doing the lecture and she demonstrated tacking up on

Suki's lovely yellow dun Twinkle and then she undid it all and told us to bring Charm and Sugar out too. So we practised tacking up on them in threes, which was cool 'cos I got to spend time hanging round with Charm and making a fuss of him without it seeming strange.

In our lesson this morning we did flat work, and Sally explained that it will help us with our jumping. Apparently the three important things you need to jump well are balance, impulsion and rhythm. I wanted to call out, "And you need a good pony who listens to you and picks his feet up!" But I didn't dare say that because Sally is quite strict most of the time and I thought she might get annoyed.

So we did all these turns and circles, and some riding straight down the centre and three-quarter lines, and we worked on making lots of transitions, which Sally says is good for impulsion. Then we started practising figures of

eight, dropping into trot and changing our
canter lead in the middle – we'll need to do
that twice when we jump the course. At first
Cracker just wanted to carry on up the track
and not come through the middle at all. Then
when I finally got him to trot through the
diagonal he refused to go back into canter, so in
frustration I tapped him with my crop.

"Get your leg on first, Chloe!" Sally called
out. "You can't just sit there and
then blame Cracker when he
doesn't canter!"

me v. flustered!

I felt really red and flustered
when she said that – I wasn't just
sitting there – to me it felt like I was kicking
away like crazy! Bella always got her canter back
as soon as she asked – and on the right leg too.
Oh, it's just so annoying! Sally probably thinks
I'm completely rubbish – if I was on Charm
she'd see that I really *can* ride, and that I *do* put

my outside leg back and everything — it's not my fault that Cracker doesn't listen to me!

I was so frustrated I made things a bit awkward in the yard after the lesson, although I didn't mean to. Bella and I had tied up our ponies next to each other to untack and give them a brush down. The ponies have their own grooming kits and each bit of the kit has the pony's name on. Well, somehow Charm's body brush had gone missing and she asked me if she could borrow Cracker's. I was about to say yes, but somehow a big "No!" came out of my mouth.

"But you're not even using it," said Georgia, looking confused.

I felt myself going all red and flushed again, like I did when Sally kept correcting me in the lesson. "But I'm just about to," I mumbled.

I wished I hadn't said no, but I didn't know how to get out of it, so I picked up the brush, planning to use it quickly then give it straight to Bella. But by that time Georgia had stepped in and lent hers, and it looked like I'd started using mine just to be awkward. Urgh!

Luckily they forgot about it over lunch and everything was fine by the time we got our fruit and yoghurt, but I can't let Bella find out how I feel about Charm – I'll have to try even harder to get over my jealousy.

Tuesday, in my room after a lovely tea of jacket potatoes with tuna and sweetcorn - yum!

Tonight we're having a table tennis tournament in the games room, and we've only got twenty mins before it starts so I'm going to have to write really fast! I'm alone up here 'cos Bella and Georgia are on washing-up duty.

Before we got our ponies out to mount up for our jumping lesson, Sally called us into the manège. The course had been set up! There were four fences completely up and four trotting poles to mark where the other ones would be. We all walked round the route and Sally explained the best approach to take for each jump and where the tricky bits might be. This is what the whole course is going to look like:

The JUMPING Course

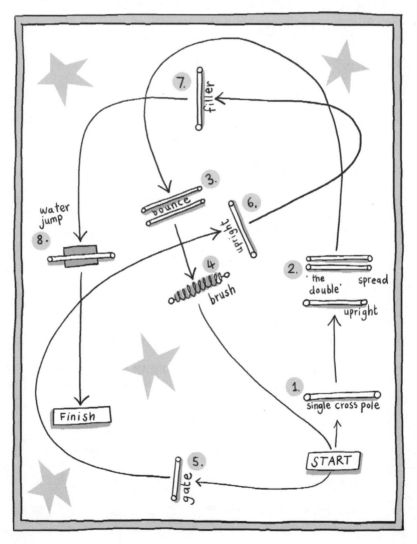

7. filler

water jump

8.

3. bounce

6. upright

4 brush

2. the double spread
upright

Finish

1. single cross pole

5. gate

START

This afternoon the only fences up were the single and spread at the start and then the bounce and brush in the middle. We had to practise going round the trotting pole (which was marking where the filler will be) to get a good approach to the bounce. I can see now why Sally was being so strict about me not letting Cracker cut the corner off in the flat work. It's a tricky turn and I'll need every inch I can get to line him up properly over these middle jumps. The thing is, you really have to hit the bounce properly because if you're too long you'll end up knocking the second bit of the fence down.

Sally said me and Millie were both still cutting the corner and she put a block there for us to go round. Tally got the message quickly, but Cracker went inside it twice and Sally made me keep doing it till I got it right. By then I had so much inside leg on I thought my calf might explode!

After ages of trying, me and Cracker finally got over the brush and back to trot in time to change canter lead (on to the correct leg at last!). We made it round the corner and over the centre of the trotting pole that marked where the gate would be.

"Honestly, Cracker," I said, as we all walked round on a long rein to let our ponies cool down, "why couldn't you just get it right in the first place? We've got so much to do before the comp – and I've had to spend an hour teaching you not to cut a corner. You're such a pest!"

"Oh, Chloe, he's not," I heard someone say. I looked up and was really embarrassed to find that Sally had heard me telling Cracker off. I went red and tried to explain. "It's just, my dad's coming on Friday and I've promised him I'll get a clear round, but Cracker won't listen to me round the corners and I'm sure he's going to knock the gate and I don't know how I'll get him back into trot in time after the brush to change canter lead and…"

I trailed off. Sally looked annoyed. "Chloe, honestly!" she cried. "Poor Cracker's doing his best! You need to work on the communication between you, and to be firmer when you ask for

Sally CROSS!

something. If you looked up and ahead more round the tight corner he'd understand what you wanted better. It's true he's not a very experienced jumper, but he tries hard and he's getting there."

"I know, but it doesn't seem fair that I have to work so hard when some of the other ponies just get it right first time and…" I began, but Sally cut me off.

We both knew who I meant by *some of the other ponies.*

41

"But you're not on the other ponies," she said firmly. "I gave Cracker to you because I thought you could bring out the best in him. I still think you can, Chloe, but you need to work together as a team and build up a partnership, like Bella has with Charm."

That really stung me.

"Just be careful that you're not so desperate to achieve a clear round in the competition that you actually stop yourself from doing it," Sally said then.

As she gave Cracker a pat and walked off I stared after her. Even thinking about it now, I still don't understand what she meant. How can I stop myself from getting something by really wanting it? That doesn't make sense.

 Oh, Millie's just come up to say the table tennis tournament's about to start. I'd better go!

Tuesday night

When we got into our beds, Bella was going on
and on about how great Charm is so I
pretended to fall asleep, and after a while she
and Georgia fell asleep too so now I can write in
here by the light of my key-ring torch.

While Bella and Georgia were playing
against each other in the table tennis
tournament I slipped off to the yard to visit
Charm. I spent ages leaning over his stable
door, stroking him and telling him how much I
wish he was my pony.

I felt a bit bad then, because Cracker hadn't been turned out yet, and I could see him in the barn, munching hay. I'm sure he saw me too – but I didn't go over and fuss him. I would have, if I'd had more time. Maybe. But I didn't really feel like it.

The table tennis was fun – Millie's older brother James organized it, with her dad. Millie actually won, but she said the second-place person should get the prize, 'cos she's here all the time and she plays a lot. So Mai won the *Spirit* DVD – when she gets back to school she's going to ask her house mistress to put it on for all the girls. She and Suki board at their school because their parents are in Japan. They must be used to not seeing their mums and dads much because they don't seem to miss them at all.

I'm not used to it though, and after I got knocked out of the table tennis tournament I was suddenly desperate to speak to Mum, so

Jody let me phone. Dad answered, as he'd just got in the door from work. The good news is that he's almost definitely coming to the gymkhana on Friday. The bad news is that he said, "So, still reckon you're on for that clear round you promised me?"

I said, "Definitely!" but my stomach was churning. Then Mum came on the telephone and I told her all the good bits of what we'd been doing this week and none of the awkward things like how jealous I feel about Bella getting Charm. I don't want her to worry that I'm not settling in here.

Anyway, I have to think positively about that clear round. There are still three days to sort out my jumping before the comp – I'll make more effort with Cracker tomorrow and hopefully everything will go well!

Wednesday, after tea

I haven't had time to write in here all day, but loads of things have happened. Our flat work lesson this morning went fine and the Pony Care lectures on feeding and points of the horse and everything were really fun. But this afternoon's jumping lesson was a disaster.

Everything has gone wrong. I mean, *really* wrong. I've fallen out with Bella and Georgia. And the worst thing of all is that it's my own stupid fault.

This afternoon when we rode into the manège all eight jumps were in place, and my stomach flipped with excitement. Before starting at the beginning, though, we did some work on the last jump, which is the water tray.

Sally explained that although it's only a single it's the most challenging fence, because ponies

46

can find the water a bit spooky. She said we'd just walk our ponies through the water first, without the pole, so they could get used to it.

Well, Charm didn't mind at all and Tally splashed straight through it. Even Prince was fine once he'd had a good look.

But not Cracker.

He walked through it on the second try, and for a moment I thought we'd be okay. But when Sally put the pole up, even at a much lower height than it will be on Friday, he just absolutely refused to go over, even in trot. He had this way of seeming like he was going over, then scampering sideways at the last minute, and it caught me out every time. After a few tries, I felt like I was holding everyone up, and I had to do the fast-blinking thing to keep myself from crying. Sally came over and explained that Cracker was finding it easier to run out because the fence is narrower. She said, "You just have to ride forward positively and look ahead to the finish. You're looking down at the water, and that's going to make him think it's scarier than it is."

I wanted to say that I was doing my best, but I didn't dare. I tried looking ahead and riding Cracker forward like Sally said, but it still didn't work. Then I got annoyed and rode him at it quite fast, and this time when he lurched to the left I came flying off on to the woodchips.

Everyone laughed. I realize now they only meant it in a friendly way but I didn't see it like that at the time. As I got up and dusted myself down I didn't look anyone in the eye. I got on again and trotted to the back of the ride, but what I really wanted to do was run indoors, get in bed and have a good cry with my head under the covers. I'd thought we'd only have to worry about the gate when it came to getting a clear round but then I realized we had to deal with the water jump as well and the whole thing just seemed hopeless. It didn't help that Charm was flying over everything without even trying and Sally kept saying, "Well ridden, Bella!".

Then things got even worse. When we tried the last couple of jumps together, I still couldn't get over the water tray. Bella offered to give me a lead so Cracker could follow Charm over, which made me feel absolutely stupid, like she was just showing off and trying to make me look silly. "No thanks, I'm fine," I mumbled, without looking at her. I know now that she wasn't being mean at all, but it's too late to take back what happened.

Anyway, Sally said it was nearly time to finish
and let us all have a pop over a single, to end on
a positive note. I didn't feel positive though, and
as we walked our ponies round on a long rein to
cool them off, I was simmering with fury at Bella.

As I dismounted on the yard, I found her right
behind me and when I saw her happy, smiling
face I just snapped. "You were only offering me

a lead to make me look
hopeless!" I hissed. "You
think you're such a
good rider, but it's only
'cos Charm's so good
that he makes you look
good too. It's not fair that
you get the easy-peasy

pony while I'm stuck with Cracker!"

And then I marched Cracker straight through
to the barn and untacked on my own, not even
waiting to hear if Bella said anything back.

I got on with brushing him down, but my heart was pounding and I felt terrible – how could I have said something so mean? Everything had gone wrong and I wanted to ring Mum and get her to drive down here and take me home.

That was when Olivia and Asha came up, looking nervous. "Bella's crying," Asha announced.

I felt like running away, but I made myself follow them back to the main yard. When I got over to Charm's stable, Georgia had her arm round Bella, and Suki, Mai and Joelle were hovering beside them, looking worried.

But before I could say anything Georgia looked up and gave me a glare so cold it made me shiver. "How could you be so mean to Bella when she was only offering you a lead to help you?" she hissed.

The younger girls all stared at me and I felt completely awful, like I wanted the ground to open up and swallow me. I realized that there was only one way to explain how I'd acted – I had to tell the truth. I took a deep breath. "Bella, I'm sorry," I began. Georgia snorted but I clenched my fists and carried on.

"The thing is, I wanted Charm," I admitted. "I've been trying not to let it show, but when I was struggling so much on Cracker, I

couldn't help thinking, if I only had Charm… I didn't want to feel jealous and I tried my best to hide it–"

But Georgia interrupted me. "It's even worse that you've pretended to be her friend all this time!" she said icily.

"But I *am* her friend!" I cried. I tried to get Bella to look at me but I only caught a glimpse of her red, tear-stained face before she buried it in Georgia's fleece again.

"It's okay, Bella, you've got real friends, forget about her," said Georgia. "Come on, you'll be okay with us lot." And with that she led Bella off towards the farm house. The others followed, giving me very cross looks. I started crying then and hurried back into the house. I tried to creep through the kitchen to get upstairs but Jody was at the sink, testing Millie on her times tables. As soon as she saw my face she made me sit down and tell her what had happened. While I was explaining it all, and trying to stop crying, I realized that I've been so focussed on Charm I haven't even given Cracker a chance. I felt like I'd been mean to *him*, as well as Bella, and that made me cry even more.

I don't blame Georgia for being so angry either. She must think I'm such a horrible person after today. "I said sorry," I sniffled, "but

I don't think Bella will want to be friends with me any more."

Millie got me some Jaffa Cakes even though it was nearly time for tea and Jody gave me a hug, saying, "I'm sure deep down Bella knows you didn't mean it. You can always try apologizing again later. Just give her time to calm down and it'll blow over, you'll see. Now how about helping me get the tea going?"

So I did, and then I set the table.

I dreaded having to face the girls at tea, but Millie sat next to me and no one said anything nasty. I tried to smile at Bella a couple of times but she still wouldn't look at me. I didn't dare smile at Georgia in case she did her icy glare and it made me start crying again.

It's so lucky my washing-up duty tonight was with Millie. After we'd cleared up, she had to carry on with her maths practice, so when I'd put everything away I just sat down next to her and got my Pony Camp Diary out and I've been writing in here ever since. I should have gone to the games room for the film, but I sort of haven't quite made it yet. There's someone else I need to say sorry to (as well as Bella), and it can't wait till tomorrow, or even one more minute.

I just went to ask Jody and she says I can go up to the field because Lydia's there, but I have to come back when she does. And Jody's given me a carrot from the fridge.

Got to go now!

Wednesday, after lights out

I'm in bed, writing by the light of my key-ring torch again. I tried to hang round in Millie's room for as long as possible after lights out, hiding under the covers at the bottom of her bed, but when Jody came up to check on us all she made me come back in here. Luckily Bella and Georgia were asleep so I didn't have to face them.

At least me and Cracker are friends now. Luckily he came when I called him over. I leaned over the fence, gave him a big pat and said sorry for being so mean, and especially for spending time with Charm when I could have been with him. I ruffled his mane and whispered, "Cracker, I'm so sorry for blaming you for our bad jumping when I should have been thinking of us as a team and riding you better and riding you more positively."

Cracker looked at me with his big black eyes, and I'm sure he understood. I added, "I've brought you a carrot to say sorry." When I held it out he munched it right up, so I know it's all okay between us now.

I wish I could just give Bella a carrot and then she'd like me again. I've just thought, maybe I should be calling her Isabella now because she is only Bella to her friends and maybe I'm not her friend any more. Urgh! I hope Jody's right and that things *will* blow over tomorrow.

Goodnight!

Thursday 11.12am, before the treasure hunt

We're just having some drinks and biscuits before we go out on the treasure hunt. My timetable from Jody has changed again today because we had our lecture first instead of the lesson. Sally said we'd need the skills for going on the treasure hunt.

I thought that meant the lecture would be on solving clues, but actually it was about road safety and first aid, and how to put boots and bandages on your pony and what to do if you get lost in the countryside. I've bandaged Cracker's legs because Sally said we might be going through the woods, and we have to be as prepared as possible. We also put our ponies' bridles on over their head collars, and each clipped a lead rope on to our D-rings so that we could dismount and have a picnic without the ponies galloping off. When I'd finished all the preparation, I made a big fuss of Cracker and told him how smart he looked.

I have sort of smiled at Isabella a couple of times and Georgia hasn't made a horrible face at me or anything so that's a bit better at least. The other girls seem to have forgotten about our falling-out because when I helped Asha to do Sugar's bandages and Olivia to put on Ebony's boots they were both chattering away to me as if nothing had happened.

Oh, hang on a sec…

Jody just called us all over to her and announced that we're being split into three teams for the treasure hunt. I'm in her team with Isabella and Joelle. When she read out the teams, she gave me a secret wink, so I know she fixed it like that on purpose so that me and Isabella will have a chance to make up. I hope we do!

Thursday 8.41pm, waiting for my turn in the shower

I have volunteered to go last so I can write in here.

Guess what? Me and Bella have made up! And guess what else? Our team won the treasure hunt! Well, one special pony in particular won it, but I'll tell you about that in a minute.

Before we left the yard on the treasure hunt, Sally gave each team a map and their first clue. She explained that there would be three

different sets of clues and three separate routes to follow, but that we would all meet up at the same final place to search for the treasure. Our team leaders had a cool saddle-bag each, packed with our sandwiches and water and the mobile and first-aid kit. Then Lydia handed out fluorescent bibs to wear over our riding clothes so we could easily be seen by any passing cars.

Sally said the only rule was that we had to stop for a half-hour lunch break so the ponies could have a rest. Our team went into the kitchen with Jody and worked out where the first clue was telling us to go, and then we got our ponies out and headed off.

Johnny's team had gone already but Sally's was still in the yard. We'd worked out that we needed to head for the church in the hamlet marked on the map. We walked along the road for a little while and then turned up a track. It was good because we all talked together and even though Bella didn't say anything exactly *to* me she wasn't ignoring me either, and after a while I

didn't feel so nervous around her. We trotted
on and when we hit a nice wide uphill bit next
to some fields we persuaded Jody to let us
have a canter, to help us get ahead of the other
teams. "Okay, then," she said, smiling. "Millie
and her dad will be dragging their team across
the countryside at high speed, so we might as
well try to compete!"

Cantering up the hill was fantastic and I
could tell that Cracker really loved being out of
the manège!

It took about half an hour to get to the
church and we found our next clue pinned to
the noticeboard in the little stone porch. I
dismounted and held Joelle's pony while she
jumped down and ran to get it. It said:

Follow the green arrows.
Stick to the path.
Be good.
Or you'll end up like Little Red Riding Hood.

"Whoever wrote this isn't very good at poems!" I said, giggling. It was nice that Bella giggled at that too.

"Oh, thanks very much!" harrumphed Jody, but she was laughing.

"*You* wrote it!" I cried. "So you must know the answer!"

She nodded, but of course she wouldn't tell us where to go next or help us with the clue at all.

So we all dismounted and huddled round the map. After a while, Bella cried, "Aha! I've got it! Little Red Riding Hood was told to stick to the path through the woods in the fairy story, wasn't she?" She pointed at the woods marked on the map. "If we ride to the edge I bet we'll find that they've put some arrows up, maybe pinned to trees. Then we'll just have to follow them through the woods. As long as we stick to the path as the rhyme says we'll find our next clue."

"Well done, Bella, that's brilliant," I said.

"Thanks," she said, smiling, but she still didn't look exactly *at* me.

Jody said, "If that's what you girls think, then let's get going!"

"But are we right?" Bella asked. Jody just made a zipping her lips sign. She wasn't giving anything away!

"What do *you* think, Cracker?" I asked, and he actually whinnied right at that moment, making everyone laugh. "Cracker thinks you're right too," I told Bella. This time when she smiled, her eyes met mine and I started to think that things might turn out okay between us.

So we set off for the woods and sure enough there was a green arrow on a post where the path entered them. We had to duck a bit under the trees at times and I was glad I'd put the bandages on Cracker, as there was a lot of bramble around. After a few more green arrows, we came out the other side on to a nice grassy bit by a field, where we found a piece of paper pinned to a tree. Our next clue!

Jody said we should have our lunch first before working it out, and even though we were keen to keep going, we were all pretty hungry too. We dismounted, took off the ponies' bridles and clipped our lead ropes to their head collars – then the ponies could have lunch too! Joelle needed the loo and Jody took her back into the wood to go in private while Bella and I held Bonny and Monsoon for them. I knew it was my chance to talk to Bella – and I took it.

It was really awkward at first and I didn't know how to begin, but then suddenly I found myself blurting it out. "I really *am* sorry I was mean to you," I gabbled. "I did want Charm but now I'm so glad I got Cracker and I'm just really,

really, *really* sorry and…" I trailed off then, not knowing what else to say. There was a horrible moment when I thought she was going to tell me to get lost and never speak to me again, but luckily she didn't. Instead she said, "That's okay, Chloe, I forgive you. And, well, you know *why* you got Cracker and not Charm, don't you?"

I shrugged. "Just the way things turned out, I suppose," I said.

"Chloe!" she cried. "Don't be dense! It's because Sally thinks you're a good rider. That's why she gave you a pony who needs more guidance."

I couldn't help but feel pleased. "Thanks," I said, "but maybe Sally thought I was a better rider than I am. I still can't get Cracker over that water jump. I'm going to have to wear a swimsuit in the comp tomorrow, because something tells me I'm going to get wet!"

Bella laughed at that and everything was okay
between us again, but we still shook hands to
make it official. By the time Jody got back with
Joelle, we were chatting away and she gave me
a secret wink and looked really pleased.

 We all sat down together and had
our lunch, which was egg
mayonnaise or ham rolls, and
bananas for after – of course,
 Cracker managed to pinch half of
mine! While we were eating we
worked out what the next clue
meant and where we should go. The piece of
paper said:

> If you take the correct path,
> The next clue you will find.
> But don't go the wrong way,
> Or you'll get left behind!

"That's not very helpful!" said Bella at first, glancing up the bridleway ahead of us, which forked into two paths. "It doesn't tell us *which* is the correct path. It's impossible!"

But I just grinned. I do crosswords with Mum all the time and they quite often say 'correct' to mean 'right', as in left and right. "It means take the right path, not the left," I explained. "'Correct' means 'right', and 'you'll get left behind' means if you take the left path you won't reach the treasure first. I'm pretty sure that's it."

"Chloe, you're a genius," said Bella, and I blushed with pride.

So we got back on our ponies and rode through the fields in walk, chatting. After ages of not finding the next clue, we got a bit worried we were falling behind the other teams, so we trotted on.

Luckily we soon found it, tacked to a fence post along the path. It said:

> Up and down
> And up again.
> Not where fish fly,
> But where birds swim.

Joelle got the giggles about that. "That's silly, birds don't swim!" she said.

"Ducks do," said Bella, smiling and pointing at the map.

There was a village with a duck pond marked on it about a mile away, and no sooner had she pointed it out than we were off. The path took us up a hill, then down a valley and up another hill, just as the clue said. We trotted as much as we could and had another canter when we came to a nice wide bit of path. Jody even let

Bella and I jump a couple of low scrubby

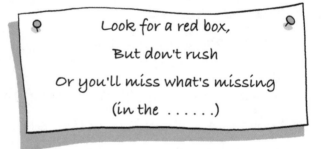

bushes, and it was so cool just doing
it for fun and not worrying about
knocked poles or clear
rounds or anything.
We got to the village
quite quickly and saw
Johnny's team so we knew the treasure was
nearby. On a post by the duck pond was our
team's final clue. It said:

> Look for a red box,
>
> But don't rush
>
> Or you'll miss what's missing
>
> (in the . . . . . .)

We didn't know what the end bit meant, but
we looked on the map and there was a red
telephone box marked in the centre of the
village. Bella and I started heading for it straight

away, but Jody called us back and made us calm
down and get in a line us girls in front of her.
She said that there would be a few cars in the
village and we had to be sensible. So we were
careful, even though we could see Johnny's
team trotting on towards the phone box and all
I wanted to do was to break into a canter and
get there first. Then we saw Sally's team come
round the corner and trot towards the church,
so we knew they were on their second to last
clue, and would find the final one at the church
somewhere.

When we got to the phone
box, Mai was holding Twinkle
for Suki. I felt disappointed
that we'd lost, but then Suki
came out empty handed!
"There's nothing in there,"
she said. "Sally's team must
have got here first."

But we told her that we'd seen them by the church, so they weren't even on this clue yet, and we were all really puzzled. Jody and Johnny just looked at each other, grinning. I knew by now they weren't going to give anything away even if we begged and pleaded. We all looked at the clue again. "It's warning us not to rush, but we all rushed to the phone box," said Mai. "Maybe we need to think again."

"How can you miss what's missing?" Bella wondered aloud.

I was confused for a moment too, but then I got it. "We mustn't miss that there's a word missing," I said. "It must be the end of the last line, because it doesn't make sense as it is. What rhymes with 'rush'?"

"Mush? Gush? Nothing!" cried Bella, getting frustrated.

I was busy trying to think of more things that rhymed with 'rush' but Cracker had other ideas.

He started wandering over to the hedge and I gathered up my reins and tried to steer him back to the group. "No, Cracker!" I told him. "Stop ignoring me! We're supposed to be a

team, remember?"

But he just stuck his head in the hedge and when I finally managed to pull him up, he was

chomping on a carrot! Well, it only took me about five seconds to realize that carrots don't grow on hedges, and I laughed out loud. "Over here!" I called out. "Cracker's found the treasure!" I leaped down and pulled a red box out of the bush, as everyone trotted up to see. There was a carrot or apple for every pony in a tray on top of the box and I had to quickly hand it up to Jody to stop Cracker from scoffing the lot!

"The missing word was 'bush!'" I told them.

"The phone box was a *red* herring, get it?" said Johnny.

"We would have got it sooner if the rhymes were better!" Mai replied, and we all giggled.

"Stop knocking the rhymes, they took me ages!" cried Jody, but she was laughing too.

"Well done, Cracker!" I said, giving him a big pat and a stroke. "You found the treasure. Clever boy!" He nuzzled my arm, so I knew he was happy too!

Sally's group caught up with us then and she asked who found the treasure. "Chloe did," said Bella, with a smile. I glanced nervously at Georgia, but she smiled at me too. She was obviously happy to forget about the falling out if Bella was – what a relief!

"Actually, Cracker found it," I said.

"It sounds like a case of excellent teamwork to me," said Sally, and I just couldn't stop grinning.

Inside the red box were three cool pony notelet and envelope sets for the winning team. We let Joelle have first choice because she's the youngest, then I picked the one with the bay Welsh Section B on, because he looked a bit like Cracker – well, not the colour but the same cheeky eyes. There were mini chocolate bars in there too, one for everyone. We all got off to stretch our legs and ate them while feeding our ponies

their prizes (except Cracker, of course, who'd already scoffed his. I made a big fuss of him though, in case he felt left out). Jody put our writing sets in her saddle-bag until we got back to the yard. Then off we went, one long string of happy riders and ponies with no falling-outs.

When we got back and untacked, I had to give Cracker's carrotty bit a good scrub under the tap. But instead of thinking *urgh what a horrible job* it felt like one of my happiest moments ever – it was so fantastic just being on the yard in the sunshine with my friends, caring for my lovely pony. I wish I could stay here for ever and never go home!

Oh, the shower's free. Bye for now!

Very early on Friday morning!

I was going to write more last night but I fell asleep. I worked out that altogether we did two hours and twenty minutes of riding on the treasure hunt – no wonder I was tired out!

I woke up early, thinking about the jumping comp. Then I crept round getting dressed, but it still wasn't time to get up so I've got back into bed in my clothes!

Me and Bella shared out our notelets between the three of us so we all have the same, because we didn't want Georgia to feel left out. Then we had a fab idea – we're going to write thank yous to the Sunnyside staff for our brilliant week at Pony Camp. I can hardly bear to think that it's our last day, it's all just gone so fast! It's the jumping comp today – I can't believe it's come so quickly. Luckily we've got another lesson to work on it this morning. I just hope there's still time to turn things round with Cracker before the this afternoon. Dad's expecting to see me get a clear round and it will be awful if I get dumped in the water tray instead!

But whatever happens, I'm really looking forward to having a good time with my friends and my fab pony. I can't wait to fetch Cracker in from the field and get going.

Oh, cool, the alarm's just gone off. I know – I'll lie down and pretend to have just woken up, then Bella and Georgia will be amazed to see me in my clothes – ha ha!

Morning break on Friday

Hurrah! We finally made it over the water jump! My gorgeous Cracker is such a star!

After we'd warmed up, we went over all eight jumps at a lowish height, to get into the swing of things. Georgia got muddled up and she and Prince went the wrong way at first, and we all had poles down – so at least I didn't feel like the only one getting in a mess.

At first Cracker wouldn't go over the water jump, but I didn't get annoyed, because I could see everyone was having their own problems. And I knew he was trying – it wasn't his fault he didn't like the look of it.

After a few goes, with him running out every time, I was getting a bit downhearted. That's when Bella offered me a lead. Of course this time I said yes please! I followed a few paces behind Charm as we went round the corner and towards the water jump. Charm popped it easily, and Cracker just followed him over, almost before he realized what he was doing! I gave him a big pat and thanked Bella loads. Sally told me to take him straight over again on my own and sure enough he jumped like a dream! I still had the gate down though, so no clear round yet. We'll just have to try really, really hard this afternoon and hope for the best.

Oh, gotta go, we're all going to tie our ponies up in the yard and make them look extra smart for the comp!

Just to quickly say...

...how gorgeous Cracker is looking! I've done
some lovely little mane plaits, all I've got to do
now is wind them up into
neat knots. I've given his coat
a really good brush and
even put some bright
blue ribbons in his tail.
Now I've just got to get into
my jodhs and sort my hair out and we're ready.

Oh, I've just looked out of the bedroom
window and our car has pulled up. Mum and
Dad are both getting out!

Friday night, snuggled up in my own bed!

Well, even though I'm not at Sunnyside Stables any more (boo!), I wanted to finish off my Pony Camp Diary by writing about what happened in the jumping comp.

It was so exciting riding into Group A's manège, which was set up as a practice area with just one jump in. We warmed up and had a couple of goes over the upright, then Sally explained that in the comp we would have two turns each, and as they wouldn't be timing us the aim was to get a clear round. We all wished each luck, and then one by one we were called into the arena, where we had to bow to the judges (who were Lydia and Johnny).

Cracker and I started off okay. We were very close on the gate, but I couldn't look back to see whether it was down. I needed all my focus to get the turn right. We came through the middle of the arena and over the upright without a hitch, and I changed my canter lead. We approached the water jump straight and in a nice rhythm, but Cracker still ran out!

I was really disappointed because I thought we'd got that sorted out this morning, but I tried to keep calm and turned him round. We'd only had one refusal. We still had another chance. I was a bit nervous though, and Cracker picked up on it, because he rushed at the jump, then swerved out again at the last minute. I managed to stay on but I felt my heart sink – we hadn't gone clear. We weren't alone though – no one had managed a clear round except for Georgia.

After I dismounted I stood fiddling with Cracker's girth for no reason, to avoid having to go over to my parents. When I saw Dad coming towards me, I was going to pretend I had something urgent to do in the tack room. But in the end I stayed put because I didn't want to miss any of my time with Cracker.

As Dad reached us, I stiffened and Cracker gave me an inquisitive look and nuzzled my arm. He could tell something was wrong. I looked up at Dad and decided to get the first word in. "Okay, so I didn't get a clear round, but so what? It's really hard, you know," I mumbled.

But instead of being cross, Dad just held his hands in the air. "Chloe, calm down!" he cried. "I think you're doing really well and so does Mum."

"But I promised I'd get a clear round, that's why you came…" I began.

"It's you who kept talking about getting a clear round," said Dad, "not me. Honestly, I just want you to enjoy yourself. We all think you're doing brilliantly."

"Really?" I mumbled.

Dad put his arm round my shoulder. "Maybe I don't say it often enough, but I'm so proud of you, Chloe," he said. I looked up at him and his eyes were twinkling. I could tell he really was.

Sally called over to us that it was time to begin round two and I got Dad to hold my other stirrup while I remounted.

"Good luck, we'll be rooting for you," he said, with a big smile on his face.

I looked over at Mum, who waved and gave me a thumbs up.

Georgia went first this time, and she had that horrid spread down, but at least she'd gone clear in the first round, so she didn't mind too much.

Bella got a clear and I expected a little bit of my old jealousy to come back, but none did. I just felt really happy for her and Charm. Millie looked very determined in this round and we were all cheering for her, but Tally picked up too much speed on the first corner, did a handbrake turn to the bounce and ended up jumping quite

long and knocking the second pole. We all gave
them a big clap, though, for a good try. Millie
didn't look remotely bothered about not going
clear. But she's lucky, she'll probably get another
chance next week!

Then it was my turn.

Everyone was cheering and clapping as I rode
by, but when I got into the arena I didn't hear a
thing. All there was in the world were me and
Cracker and the jumps. I remembered to look
up and ahead and concentrate on where we
were going this time, and I just let Cracker get
on with jumping.

We started off a bit messy over the cross pole
and spread, but everything stayed up (phew!) and
we got into a good rhythm round the nice wide
arc at the top of the arena, which set us up much
better for the bounce and brush. We got over the
middle jump without a hitch but I only let myself
be pleased for a split second, then refocussed and

asked Cracker to trot to change our canter lead. Then we were off round the tight bend and over the dreaded gate. This time Cracker seemed to know it was a danger zone and did a huge leap over, more than clearing it. He started getting really excited after that, but I kept him nice and steady round the bend and over the upright. Then we were setting ourselves up for the water jump. I consciously breathed out and sank into the saddle. I had to let Cracker know I was relaxed, and then he would be too. I looked up and ahead at the finish, as if the jump wasn't even there, and before I knew it we were over!

We'd done it – a clear round!

Mum and Dad were cheering like crazy and I rode out of the arena grinning from ear to ear.

In the practice area I leaped off and made a huge fuss of Cracker – what a total star pony! And what a fab team we'd made!

All us Group B girls said a big well done to each other and as I was walking Cracker back into the yard, my parents came up to meet me. Mum gave me a hug and Dad said, "Well done, Chloe, that was excellent."

When we'd put our ponies back in their stables for a rest, us Group B girls got our drinks and biscuits from the kitchen, then we all sat at the edge of the other manège together to watch the younger girls play some gymkhana games. It was great fun and we cheered wildly for all of them.

Then later there was a prize-giving and we brought our ponies out again and collected our

 rosettes. I felt so proud of the clear round. And I felt even prouder that me and Cracker did it as a team – together.

I tied the rosette on to his bridle and Dad took some pictures of our group and our ponies all together, and then we asked Lydia to take one of my whole family with Cracker in the middle. Cracker nuzzled Mum's arm and she looked a bit nervous in case he nibbled her sleeve!

When it was all over, I led Cracker to the barn. I gave him a carrot I'd scrounged from Jody and spent ages fussing and stroking him while I brushed him down.

I felt upset about leaving him, but I'm planning to go back next year – I'm already trying to persuade Mum to book it! It was really sad saying goodbye to Bella and Georgia. Dad took loads of photos of us three though, and I'm going to send some to them tomorrow, with my first letter.

We've all promised to write to each other using the pony paper and envelopes!

Just as we were heading to the car with all our bags we remembered the thank-you letters we'd written, which were in my bag. I heaped all my stuff on to Dad and ran back over to the yard. Sally was there in the office so I gave her the letters.

As she opened hers, her face lit up. "Oh thanks so much, Chloe, that's very kind of you!" she said. "Thank the other girls for me, won't you?"

I nodded and made for the door. "Chloe," she said then, and I whirled round in the doorway. "You've really turned it around this week," she told me. "I'm so proud of you, well done."

I couldn't help beaming. "Thanks, but it was all down to Cracker!" I said, and I skipped out and across the yard.

I really learnt a lot at Pony Camp, and not

new friends, met some fab ponies and found out what a true partnership is – all thanks to Cracker!

Hey, I've just realized that Sally was right – when she warned me not to be so desperate to achieve my goals that it actually stopped me succeeding I didn't really understand what she meant. But I do now. As soon as I started to relax and work as a team with Cracker, we did so much better – and I had a lot more fun, too! How funny that nearly all week I thought I had to teach *him*, but actually he's taught *me* loads!

Now, I wonder which pony I'll get next year?!

Have you read?

978-1-84715-006-6   978-1-84715-007-3

Coming in June 2007:

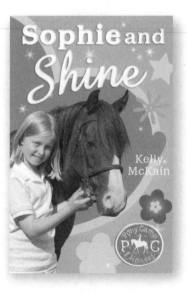

978-1-84715-020-2

To George, with love - thanks for all those
trips to Redwings Horse Sanctuary!

With special thanks to our cover stars,
Chelsea and Dusty, pony guru Janet Rising,
star instructor Jody Maile and all
at Ealing Riding School.

STRIPES PUBLISHING
An imprint of Magi Publications
1 The Coda Centre, 189 Munster Road, London SW6 6AW

A paperback original
First published in Great Britain in 2007

Text copyright © Kelly McKain, 2007
Illustrations copyright © Mandy Stanley, 2007
Cover photograph copyright © Zoe Cannon, 2007

ISBN-13: 978-1-84715-014-1

Printed and bound in Belgium by Proost

4 6 8 10 9 7 5 3

Kelly McKain

Stripes